I0618488

YUKI'S LUCK

A NOVELLA

JA'NESE DIXON

PUBLISHING

ALSO BY JA'NESE DIXON

READ THE SERIES

Yuki's Luck (Book 1)

Asher's Sonnet (Book 2)

Smith Surprise (Book 3)

When It Comes to Love (The Complete Series)

YUKI'S LUCK. Copyright © 2018 by Ja'Nese Dixon

All rights reserved.

This is a work of fiction. All of the characters, organization and events portrayed in this story are either products of the author's imagination or are used fictitiously.

No part of this book may be reproduced in any form or by any electronic or mechanical means, including information storage and retrieval systems, without written permission from the author, except for the use of brief quotations in a book review.

Warning: The unauthorized reproduction or distribution of this copyrighted work is illegal. Criminal copyright infringement, including infringement without monetary gain, is investigated by the FBI and is punishable by up to 5 years in prison and a fine of $250,000.

ISBN-13: 978-0-9987811-5-0 (paperback)

TABLE OF CONTENTS

I dedicate this book to my beta readers Franki, Sarah, and Sheila. Each step I take in pursuit of my dream is made possible by people like these amazing women. Thank you ladies!

ABOUT YUKI'S LUCK

He's stolen her heart,
it'll take luck to get it back.

JUST HER LUCK, ONE EVENING AFTER TOO MANY shots, Yuki wakes naked tangled in Dylan's expensive sheets. Yuki Smith doubts her mother's judgment on men, life, and definitely on naming her "lucky."

Dylan Jameson is her twin's best friend and all the things she's not. Filthy rich, focused, and drop-dead gorgeous. And beneath it all he is a really great guy. Then he messed it all up by asking for what she could not give, commitment.

Dylan heads to Ireland, somehow he took her *luck* with him. Now Yuki must board a plane to god-knows-where, to encounter god-knows-what, hoping for a chance to tell Dylan the truth. Because he's captured her heart and something tells Yuki she'll need *luck* to get him back.

CHAPTER 1

"Put up your mugs."

I reach for the heavy crystal tankard mug, extending it across the table towards my twin brother, Asher Smith, careful not to let my eyes slide to his left. He sent a cryptic text message.

It's on!!! Meet me at the spot in an hour.

I finalized the email I was typing, told my assistant to forward my calls to my cellphone, and now here I am in a bar at three pm with Asher, his wife Jazz, short for Jasmine, and his best friend and business partner Dylan Jameson—the one I'm avoiding in public. It's complicated.

"What are we celebrating? And hurry cause I'm hungry." I ask as my heart warms, pride does not start to explain the feelings tumbling in my chest. The smile on his face tells me it's good, really good. But I use this moment to give him a hard time. I mean, isn't that what sisters are for?

"Patience is a virtue." Asher says over his glass.

"Bite me, kid brother." I kick him. *That'll wipe that smug look off his face.*

"Ouch! And you're wearing those god-awful pointy heels." The gang laughs. I lift my legs to avoid the sweeping motion of his foot as he tries to return my sisterly love tap.

"Children, children," Dylan chimes in, "stop teasing. Get to it. I have plans." And I break my rule as my eyes meet his. Always the mediator. His strawberry blond hair, piercing blue eyes, and his wicked smile. He winks, and my heart skips a beat. Everything about him reads off limits. But like a child fascinated by the fire, I reach for the flames praying I don't get burned. Not my smartest move.

The waiter returns with our standard order of spicy wings, seasoned fries, and Dylan's insisted upon house salad on the table. And we're still waiting on the reason for this gathering in the middle of the day.

Jazz sits her mug down places her elbows on the table turning towards Dylan. "It must be a woman. For you to pass on wings and beer—"

"And the salad—" He adds.

"We all know ain't nobody touching that tired

salad but you. Who goes to a sports bar for salad?" Asher looks thoroughly confused.

"Asher, focus." I cut through their banter. "What happened to the toast? Y'all are the worst." I reach for a wing and Jazz, my hopeless romantic sister-in-law, smacks my hand and the slippery chicken tumbles to the table. "Ouch."

"That's for kicking my husband." She winks and has the nerve to laugh.

"Thanks, babe." Asher leans over the table and kisses her dismissing the raised mugs in the air, our food getting cold, and the ticking clock.

"Get a room. Make the toast already cause this mug is heavy." I retrieve my wing praying the five-second rule applies. Dylan drops his head chuckling.

"Okay, okay. We closed on a space for Smith & Jameson."

"What?" I spring to my feet, and my wing flies across the room. "Sorry," I say to no one in particular as I round the table, pulling Asher into a hug. "I knew it. I knew you would get it."

Asher and Dylan were finding it difficult to secure a location for their international beer garden and eatery. They wanted a space near downtown but roomy enough for at least six truck vendors to park and offer food. But finding adequate space stalled their brilliant plan.

"Your call did it." Asher said.

I pull back placing my hands on his cheeks. "No, your business plan did it. I'm just doing my part."

"My good luck charm." He whispers under his breath for only us to hear. I hate when he calls me that, and he knows it. "Don't give me that look." He holds up a finger. "Let me have this moment. Please."

"Okay." I reluctantly agree.

"Thank you." He kisses my cheek, the joy dancing in his eyes is infectious. I feel a silly grin matching his spread across my face.

"You're welcome." I go back to my seat, we lift our mugs with more vigor this time.

From struggling to this. I'm Vice President at BrandShare and up for a major promotion to partner. He's independently wealthy from his business ventures, and he's on course to build a legacy with the Smith name on it. I look over at Asher, certain it will only get better.

"In the words of William Shakespeare, 'It is not in the stars to hold our destiny but in ourselves'. My destiny is connected to each of you and I'm a blessed man." He smiles at Jazz as she brushes away a tear. "This toast is to my beautiful wife, talented and uber-wealthy best friend, and my *twin*."

"And Momma," I add. "Don't forget Momma."

"Never." Asher's head drops for a brief second and

when he looks up again, his eyes are glistening with unshed tears. "I will not fail with odds stacked so perfectly in my favor. We have a prime location in downtown Austin, the vendors, forty-nine of the fifty craft breweries on board, and in three days we're off to Ireland to secure a deal with one final brewery."

Dylan places a hand on Asher's shoulder. "Man we got this."

He nods. "Let's toast to Smith & Jameson Beer Garden. That we get the final contract with Impose Brew and we open our doors to the public by the summer. To Smith & Jameson."

We repeat as our mugs chime reflecting the excitement swirling around our table. I tap Asher's glass. Then Jazz. Then Dylan, and our eyes hold longer than they should. I'm frozen. The sounds in the bar and of Asher and Jazz talking cease to exist. He mouths, *Don't be late.* I look back and forth to ensure no one saw it but me. He smiles and I find the strength to pull from his vortex.

We pass the time drinking beer, eating wings, and Dylan steps away to take a call and Jazz heads to the ladies room.

"When will BrandShare make their partnership decision?" Asher asks.

"Soon. They usually announce it by now, I don't know what the hold up is." I lick the spicy sauce from my fingers. I push around the contents on the messy table searching for the little wet towelettes. "I inked a deal for $5 million dollars yesterday. I'm just hoping that's enough."

"That should guarantee your offer." He finishes off the fries passing me a napkin.

"I hope so."

BrandShare is a boutique marketing firm I joined after graduate school. My department specializes in subscription boxes. I pair companies with products as a means of expanding their presence in the market-place and increasing brand recognition. My clients range from high-end cosmetic companies to custom chocolatiers. I'm on track to making partner by my twenty-seventh birthday less than two weeks away.

Waiting for them to announce it is killing me. Then it hits me. "What if—"

"Don't worry. They're slow, not stupid."

"Brother you are totally biased." I smile appreciating his unwavering confidence in me.

"Damn right. Join Smith & Jameson, we can use that marketing brain of yours." He leans forward, I shake my head. That's not an option.

"One Smith is more than enough to secure the legacy. Besides, I have a job." I try to sound noncha-lant about it. Sure it has become more of a grind than a passion, becoming a partner would give me more

control of the clients I work with and inject some
excitement back into my career.

"It's not only about *our* legacy. This is our family
business." His knowing eyes scan my face, and I
glance away. "Is that the only reason you won't accept
my offer?"

The beer garden is their business. And the rest of
his statements sounds like the Charlie Brown teacher
in my head as I see *him*.

"You two think y'all have us fooled." I hear
through the haze. "We all know you guys are
attracted to each other." He motions across the room
towards Dylan talking with another woman. "Just get
together already and save us the awkward tension."

"There's no *together* for me. And *what* tension?" I
roll my eyes, over this conversation. "BrandShare,
you, Momma, that's more than enough for me."

"Being alone sucks." Asher states.

"I'm not alone I have you."

"Big sis, I pray you find a man truly worthy of
how precious you are." His eyes pierce through my
facade and hit his intended target—my fragile heart.

"Yeah right. I'm the ball buster, remember?" I
laugh. His grimace says he's not buying it. "My hands
are full. Partnership. Your spot. And who knows I
may finally take up a hobby."

I look over again, Dylan is retrieving his phone

from the gorgeous petite blonde. He drops it in his pocket. *Player.* I need to get out of here. I find the wet wipes and clean the remaining sauce off my hands as Jazz returns, her face tense. I turn a questioning gaze to Asher, his face clearly reads, *Don't ask.*

"I'm out. I want to stop by my office before heading home." I toss the dirty wipe on my plate grabbing my purse from the back of my chair. "Congratulations again."

"Babe, I'll be back." Asher stands as I do.

"Stay here. I'm fine." I motion for him to sit back in his eat. "My car's right across the street."

"I'm walking Yuki to her car." He talks over me, kissing Jazz's check. Then he places a hand on my lower back guiding me to the front door.

"Good night Jazz," I call over my shoulder. "See you Sunday." *Call me*, I mouth. She nods, I send her air kisses. "Love you."

The sports bar is near capacity. Which isn't a surprise since they have Friday night half-off Happy Hour. I maneuver around people, tables, and chairs, finally reaching the exit. "What's that all about?"

"We're in a rough patch. I hope getting this trip behind us will relieve some of the stress and get us back to honeymooning." He opens the door, and I step out into the chilly evening.

"Is there anything I can do?"

"Nah, you've done more than enough. I predict…." Stopping next to my car, I turn with a smile. We've played this game since we were kids and now my very grown, very handsome brother is once again predicting our future.

"Oh, brother." I roll my eyes. "You do recall that you get it wrong about one hundred percent of the time. I appreciate your tenacity." I pinch his cheeks.

"Such a hater." He flicks his hand in my direction like he's shooing a fly away. He chuckles shoving his hand in his pockets, then he pulls me against him. Together we lean against my car as if our destiny is written in the Austin skyline.

"Did you ever think we'd be here?" He asks so low I almost miss it.

"Like physically? Against my car, in a parking lot?" The sun is dropping, and the breeze is perfect.

"Are you charging for these terrible jokes? Because you are laying it on heavy tonight." I dig my elbow into his side. He folds over laughing. "No, smarty pants, our lives."

"Never. Do you think it will get better?" I rest my head against his shoulder, his head now resting on top of mine.

"I know it will."

"Then tell me, oh wise one. What do you predict?" I trust very few people in my life, and this man is one of them. If he says the sky will be purple in the morning, I will bank on it. Only one other man comes close, *Dylan*.

The sound of chatter rings through the air as if the bar door was opened and closed. I glance toward the door, and there's Dylan. He taps the face of his watch and disappears.

I wonder if Asher noticed but he continues, "This time, two weeks from today, our lives will change for the better. You will be 27. You will be the first female partner at BrandShare. Smith & Jameson will secure the contract with Impose Brew and my marriage…" his voice drops.

"Will resume the honeymoon," I finish for him, placing my hand on his chest. I kiss his cheek, disarming my car doors. "It'll work out, you'll see."

He glances down into my eyes, and a faint smile crosses his face. I squeeze his arm and lower inside my car. "When are you telling Momma?"

"Let's do it in the morning. Meet me over there. We'll go to breakfast."

"Cool. I'll be there around nine. Love you."

I sit in my car staring at Asher's retreating back. Images of Dylan chatting with that petite blonde hanging on to his every word. What am I doing? Comparing myself to the blonde?

No.

Maybe.

Flipping down my visor, I touch up my lipstick, and my mother's face stares back. I slap it closed and try to scrub my thoughts clear of any comparisons to her. I pull the visor open again.

"Yuki, you control your destiny. You are a partner. No more secret meetings with Dylan. No more comparing yourself to petite blondes. No more Dylan." *I said that already.* I close the visor and rest my head on the steering wheel. It can't hurt to say it a few more times. "No more Dylan, no more Dylan, no more Dylan."

CHAPTER 2

"Do you have a reservation?" A man in a penguin suit asks from behind a podium. I glance over his shoulder, and the inside is formal with white linen and soft candles. It echoes one sentiment, romantic.

No more Dylan. No more Dylan. No more Dylan. This chant isn't working as images of his smile, his eyes and a low rate hum ensue. The one I get every time I think about him. Every time I see him. It happens more frequently. This romantic dinner will not help.

Before Asher married Jazz the three of us did everything together. Then our three became two. It felt odd without Asher at first. Over the past year, it became something we did. Every Saturday. Movies. Museums. Concerts.

Missing our third wheel this time alone feels intimate. And although our secret meetings aren't really a secret we have never had a candlelight dinner. But this is the address he sent by text this morning.

"Ma'am." His annoyed glare bores into me.

"Ah, Jameson, Dylan Jameson." He scans the list under a reading lamp, my stomach's in knots.

"Dylan, what are you doing?" I whisper searching the room for his familiar face.

"I want to celebrate your birthday." His silky voice holds a challenge. I stumble back connecting with his chest.

"We shouldn't." Dylan steps closer planting his large hands on my hips.

"Of course we should."

"Sir." The suit insists.

"Give us a second." Dylan turns me to face him as he scans my body from head to toe. A singe of heat accompanies his roaming appraisal of my black dress paired with silver heels. "Yuki. Join me. Or I could celebrate your birthday alone." I see his smile before his head falls.

"How do you plan to celebrate my birthday without me?" I punch him in the arm. "You don't have to do this." I glance again over his broad shoulders at the impatient suit.

"I know how important twenty-seven is to you."

I don't buy *luck*. However, on my seventh birth-day, Momma adopted me. I graduated college at seventeen. Twenty-seven looks as promising as the others. This is the downside of knowing him for most of my life. There are very few secrets between us. I stare up into his blue eyes, and I shiver.

"We *could* dine upstairs," he offers.

Taking a deep breath. Upstairs means fewer eyes, we would be alone. Alone, *alone*. But this is Dylan, we've spent time alone before. I roll my shoulders back and close the space between us.

"What's upstairs?"

"My penthouse suite." His smoldering eyes are melting my resolve to treat him like a brother. Hell, I've known him since we were seven. Nothing about this man mirrors his seven-year-old self except maybe the honesty hidden in the depths of his eyes. And memories, really great memories.

The suit clears his throat a few times, and Dylan glances back with a raised brow. And the suit nervously walks away to seat a couple.

"What do you say?" Dylan asks.

As a marketer and a saleswoman, I close deals. It is what I do. I tell colorful tales, full of hope and potential fused with a dedicated focus. I am a visionary. I see the unseen. I get paid millions to do it. But this is hard to envision. I can't see how this will end.

How can our friendship remain intact? How will Asher feel if it all blows up in our faces? If Dylan learns….

"Dinner. Drinks." He restates casting his own vision for tonight.

"*Just* dinner and drinks."

"Baby girl, we passed just dinner and drinks a long time ago. I want more. Much more. You know it. I know." He pauses letting his words penetrate my apprehension. "But I'll accept what you offer."

I bite the inside of my lip counting the cost. "So dinner, drinks, and—"

"You in my bed beneath me."

The air swooshes from my lungs. His intense gaze melting through my objections. And then his mouth covers mine. In front of the suit, the other waiting patrons. Soft and persuasive. His large hands grip my waist pulling my body to his. Intense, yet familiar.

Our first kiss.

He pulls back. "Yes?"

I swallow, my body swims with desire at seeing this Dylan for the first time. "Yes."

Dylan grabs my hand as if we've done it a million times before guiding me through the lobby with nonchalant grace. *Am I really going to his place?*

He stops in front of the elevator and presses the up arrow. I use the time to catch my breath and return his assessing gaze. His polished shoes and suit are expensive. The soft sheen of the navy blue fabric against his olive skin paired with a crisp white shirt and a power red tie. He screams wealth. But its the full beard trimmed low that imparts the right amount of edge to his pristine appearance.

I'm glad I picked my best black dress. The knit fabric hugs my curves with a plunging v in the front, the back is open with double straps. It's what I call sexy in the front, vixen in the back. I straightened my bra strap length hair and adorned a smokey dark eyeshadow look with ruby red lipstick.

"Yuki you look gorgeous tonight." He leans against the wall, powerful with his arms crossed over his massive chest.

Ding.

The elevator doors open and his hand finds my lower back. A hiss escapes under his breath. I glance over my shoulder meeting his gaze. Dylan is taller than my brother by at least two inches. I feel like a smaller woman in their presence, which is rare for my five-foot eleven-inch height.

"Where's the rest of your dress, Miss Smith?" His eyes dance with mischief.

"Do you not approve Mr. Jameson?" The ease of

our normal banter settles between us as the elevator doors close. I spin around to face him. The sparks in his eyes thrill me while my attraction for him bubbles to the surface terrifying me. Feelings I've run from my entire life.

Love is not in for me. I am the evidence of love going terribly wrong. My veins hold conflicting truths fusing my parents and severing me from my living relatives residing in Korea. My black father and Korean mother banked on love and lost.

He presses the PH button and enters a code on the keypad. The doors close. We are alone. He takes two giant steps, his eyes zero in on my silver body necklace. His index finger runs the length from my neck, down my chest, between my breasts. I inhale his familiar scent.

"Why is this the first time you've invited me to your place?" I ask.

"I had to wait for the right time."

"For what?"

"For you to hear me out." His voice low and smooth speaks volumes as his large hand brushes my exposed skin then rests on my bottom.

"Why now?"

Ding.

The open living room is massive overlooking

downtown Austin. The room is lit by the surrounding buildings and the glow from his private rooftop pool. I walk to the glass.

"Breathtaking."

"I agree." His eyes are on me.

"Dylan..." He steps closer, pulling me into his arms. "Are you sure this is wise?"

"Only one way to find out," he kisses me slow, and it leaves me trembling with need. The intimate rhythm of his tongue invades my mouth in the sweetest way, I grip the lapels of his jacket until his chest is against mine.

"Let's order dinner." I watch his eyes darken from sky blue to a vibrant hue dark enough to resemble denim.

My lips ache for a repeat , I've waited a lifetime for this moment. Before I lose my courage, I stand on my tip toes brushing my mouth against his wrapping my arms around his neck. His strong arms circle my back and lava flows through my veins to the parts that make me female.

"What do you want to eat?" His heated whisper brushes my ear, kissing my temple.

"You," escapes before I can stop it. My body aching for him to extinguish the fire he started. Not with food. But him.

"Yuki don't say it like that baby," he growls. "Dinner first. Then your gift." The promise lingering in his eyes makes the ache between my thighs intensify. He pulls me from the window to the couch. "I'll grab the menu."

I collapse on the couch.

"Make yourself at home," he says over his shoulder, loosening his tie with one hand. He walks through a door on the far end of the room. "I'll be right back."

The chant of no more Dylan is dead, its morphed into *more Dylan, please Dylan*. His kisses serve as a perfect distraction. But this is not what I need, not right now. I need to focus on getting that corner office.

I glance at the doorway hearing him move around in the back room. The open space of the living room bleeds into the dining area. Across the room, I catch a glimpse of my younger self. I walk over and see the wall lined with pictures of us over the years.

Elementary. Middle school. High school. Vacations. Each picture with Asher between us. Except one. I recognize the background, we were at Zilker Park for an outdoor concert. I am smiling at the camera, and Dylan's eyes are focused on me in the same intense gaze I saw tonight.

Has he always felt this way?

I look at the doorway anxious for his return then back at the pictures. His kisses open a hidden door I locked away years ago. A yearning I recognized for the first time our sophomore year of high school.

Asher and Dylan had a pool party at Dylan's place. As always, his parents were off traveling the world, and Momma made Asher take me along. I promised to keep quiet as long as they paid for my summer camps. But what I really wanted was a pair of diamond rings. Camps won out. They were the sensible, more affordable option, and I'd gain credits for college.

I found a spot by the pool with a book and several brochures for camps hosted around Austin, landing on a business management and entrepreneurship camp at the University of Texas. It was perfect. I circled the fee, deadline, and the website to submit my application. Satisfied I grabbed my potato chips and a Coke ready to read. Then I saw him. Really saw him.

Dylan strolled out of the house with an air of confidence that belied his fifteen years of life. Shirt off, smiling and whispering in Amber's ear. She laughed every time he leaned in, her hair blowing in the wind. I wanted more than anything to be one of the other girls.

The girls that Dylan smiled at. The girls that

Dylan whispered in their ears, giving his time. To be Dylan's girl. But he didn't see me as a girl or a young woman but as Asher's sister.

Until tonight.

CHAPTER 3

"I THINK I SHOULD APOLOGIZE FOR HAVING YOU dress up to eat Mexican food in my living room." We ordered dinner, and he made margaritas, my favorite. I'm stuffed and satisfied.

"This is perfect." He's on the cushion next to me. His thigh lightly resting against mine. I pour Dylan a shot of tequila.

"Have you heard back from Jack?" He throws it back and pours me another.

I shake my head with the glass approaching my mouth. No Jack, my boss, has not made the announcement and time is ticking. I set goals. I achieve them. It's my MO.

He downs another shot and turns to me with agitation across his beautiful face. "You've earned them billions. You'll get the promotion." His faith in my work never falters. "We all know you live for BrandShare. They'd be fools *not* to give you the position."

"Yeah." This is one of those moments when I wish I were one of the guys. And Dylan could understand how I can do the work to earn the position, yet not get the position.

Dylan is one of *the boys*. Not at my office, of course, but in life. The type of man with a commanding presence that appeals to both men and women. Men want to associate with him, women want him in their beds. Hell, he got me in his house without breaking a sweat.

BrandShare provides the clients, I close the deals with a massive one-two punch. I devote all my time —on the clock and off—to my clients. As a result, I return to my beautifully furnished home day after day, night after night, alone. Dylan's right, Brand-Share is my life.

But I'm not one of the guys. They golf. They entertain executives at strip clubs. There is only so much I can do. To offset all of their male bonding I work my ass off, bringing a unique eye, creativity, and my willingness to go the extra mile.

It's my edge. My superpower. But this wait seems different.

I gave it my all. What if my all isn't enough? I down another shot.

I'm asking my bosses to step outside the mold and bring on a female, biracial partner. The youngest in the history of the firm. *If* they decide, no, *when* they decide to make the offer I will be the first Black, first Korean, first woman and first partner under the age of thirty in one swoop.

Are they ready to take that on? Take me on? What if they give the corner office and partnership to Eric? I throw back another shot with Dylan's knowing eyes watching me.

"How can you drink this, it burns?" My throat is on fire, and I'm ready to change the subject. "That's the last one for me." He laughs as I lean an arm against the back of the couch, every muscle in my body relaxed. I turn to him curling my feet beneath me. "I recall you mentioning a gift."

"I'll go grab it." He sits forward then leans across and kisses me. "Don't move."

"I wouldn't think of it." He's relaxed with several buttons undone and his signature decorative socks. He always dressed to rival the best high-end model yet on his feet he always has the funkiest socks. He probably owns thousands. He disappears into a room off to the side and returns just as quick.

"It's not what you think it is, but it's not what it

may look like." I raise a brow at his cryptic spill. Dylan sits on the edge of the couch with a small box in the palm of his hand, there's a hopeful glint in his eyes. I smile at his nervous laugh.

"I remember one summer. We were, I don't know, sixteen or so." Running a hand over his face and then through his hair. "Anyway, you blackmailed us—"

"I what?" My mind spins as the little black box rests between us.

"You blackmailed us. Do you know how much we paid for those summer camp fees? Hell, I think you owe me at least ten thousand dollars." He's probably right.

"Cry baby cry, wipe your weeping eyes." I hold my stomach laughing. "Open it."

"Just a second." He holds a hand up, laughing with me. "You saw a jewelry catalog and there was a pair of earrings." He faces me and opens the box, diamond studs sparkle against the velvet.

I can't stop smiling as I hold back tears. I'm not the crying type, but he remembered.

"I saved all summer," he removes an earring from the box, "after paying off my blackmailer."

I slap his arm. He removes my hoop earring and places it on the table. Then he adds the diamond stud. I recall his words wrapping my hands around his wrist. "Dylan, how long have you had these?"

He breaks eye contact reaching for the other earring. "Ten years."

My heart skips a beat, or two.

"Dylan." I grab his face enjoying the tickle of his beard beneath my hands. I hear warning sounds in my head, but his eyes quiet the voice. I capture his mouth in a deep kiss and our tongues dance as I try to satisfy the unquenchable thirst resurfacing with his confession.

Ten years.

A desire I tucked away, long ago, when all I wanted was to be Dylan's girl.

His strong arm snakes around my waist pulling me across the couch in a cocoon of tequila and Dylan. Strong, bold, protective. Not aggressive, yet not passive as his mouth introduces me to the man behind my childhood fantasies. I wrap my arms around his neck, not wanting the slightest gap between our bodies, crushing my now aching breast against his rock hard chest. My fingers rake through his hair as I find myself flat on my back and the heat in the room increases, igniting a fire guaranteed to change everything between us.

His kisses move from my moist mouth to the hollow of my neck. And he uses his tongue to retrace the steps his fingers traveled down my body necklace leaving a trail to the infirmary between my thighs. I shift slightly, and he's perfectly nestled between my legs.

"Baby girl…." It sounds like a mix of a growl and a plea. Dylan pushes up and hangs over me, our breathing in sync—rapid, heavy, thick. The denim blue in his eyes gives me a clear indication that he is affected by our kissing too. His eyes snap closed.

The thought of having this well-controlled man on the brink of losing it increases the rhythm of my heart several notches. To see him mature from wimpy kid to awkward preteen, to dashing teen, now he is an irresistible man that I should leave alone. But his messy hair and flush moist skin make it hard to say no.

I run my hands up his chest. My fingers slightly shaking as I unfasten the small buttons on his shirt. His large hands massage my inner thighs as his fingers brush my satin panties, my back arching encouraged by the slightest touch from him.

I yank the hem of his dress shirt and undershirt free, reaching for his belt and he sits back with his head facing the ceiling. My brain is mixed with need and tequila, and neither want this feeling to end. Not without completion.

"Why'd you stop?" I sit up and rest on my elbows. My dress is around my hips and we look like the most scandalous picture.

"It is the hardest thing I've had to do. In life." His eyes find mine and I believe him. Knowing I placed that look in his eyes only makes me more eager to continue. I reach for his pants and notice the obvious bulge and smile up at him. "Don't look at me like that."

"Like what?" I tease. "Are we not celebrating my birthday?"

"Yes. We are."

"And, am I not the birthday girl?"

"Technically—"

"Yes or no Mr. Jameson." I slide my hands beneath his undershirt and I hear that heavenly groan again. It is lighting fuel to my fire.

"Yes," he says between clenched teeth. I run my hands over his washboard abs and his manhood jumps in my direction. I giggle. And he growls again.

"We're celebrating. I'm the birthday girl. I want you to finish what we've started."

"Baby girl I ain't what you're used to, I play for keeps."

His gaze shifts from agony to predatory and my inner voice is telling me to *pull down your dress and run!*

"So before I ruin your beautiful dress and erase your memory of any man you've ever been with, count the cost."

"Mr. Jameson," I lean forward, "that sounds like a threat."

The storm raging in his eyes should warn me that playing with this man is a no-no but the chance of him losing control, with me, makes me feel risky. And the only clear thought I can pluck from my discombobulated mind is, *for keeps* means I'd finally be Dylan's girl.

Either this is exactly what I've always wanted or I need to stay far far away from tequila. Or both.

"Let me help you decide." Dylan crawls up my body until I'm flat on my back again. He anchors a hand over my head and the other briefly brushes my panties before slipping past the elastic. His thumb finds the source of my ache, I squeeze my thighs trying to back away. "Oh no, you don't."

I reach for his shirt to hold on to anything for leverage as my heels dig into the couch. And then a finger slips in.

"Dylan—"

"No, baby girl, this is what you wanted. Isn't it?"

I nod like a maniac as the intensity increases. The feeling of tiny marching ants leaving little love bites on my exposed skin. His fingers rock inside me and his thumb massages the button granting access to ecstasy and I. Can't. Breath.

Gasping. Begging. Pleading. My vibrato quickly

turns to putty in his skilled hands. Gripping fistfuls of his shirt I ride as if my life depends on it. And then with some sort of witchery, he pushes my dress aside and latches on to my right breast. It stings just right urging me closer to the edge of the cliff.

"Ride it, baby. Give in to it." His mouth brushes against my ear casting a spell over my body as he strokes me. Deeper, and deeper. I'm on the brink of free falling and I tell him so.

"Baby that will be the sweetest gift." He bites my nipple and everything goes white as heat courses through my body. No stars. No moon. Just Dylan. And I surrender, screaming his name right before his mouth captures my hoarse cry.

What was that? And can we do it again?

CHAPTER 4

DYLAN LAYS WITH HIS BACK AGAINST THE COUCH and pulls me to his chest. His strong arm around my waist and I feel the evidence of his arousal. I glance over my shoulder. His eyes are still denim blue. I never noticed how they change until tonight.

I wiggle my bottom, he nips the sensitive space at the base of my neck. I want to ask why he stopped. Should I? I turn in a little circle until we are chest to chest. I can only imagine how I appear with my dress pushed up and the halves of the top open exposing my breast. But at this moment I don't care.

"Why'd you stop?" His olive skin looks sun-kissed a slight contrast with my own honey complexion.

"Yuki, I want nothing more than to make you completely mine. But not until you're ready." He runs a hand through my hair lightly scratching my scalp.

"Don't complicate this." He's a man with too many options and I'm a woman too grown to believe he'll settle for one woman.

"Yuki Smith you've never settled in anything. Your education, your career. Yet you're willing to settle with your heart."

"Settle? How is enjoying my time with you settling?" He remains silent and I search his eye for a sign that I'm getting through to him, so I push. "So, you mean to tell me you'll go home with that little blonde without batting an eye."

"Calm down."

"Don't tell me what to do. Explain it to me, Dylan. You flirt and tease and invite others to your bed with no strings attached." I move to sit up, my volume increasing. I yank back and hope the ball buster in me will get me out of his arms and far away before I give in.

"Baby girl your theatrics won't get you anywhere. You and I both know you are not those other women. Those other women only get a piece of my time because you want to play games."

"Games? I got your games." I cut my eyes and roll them with all the sister girl attitude I can muster. I push against the brick wall he calls a chest. "I need to go."

"You're not going anywhere until we resolve this."

"Yeah right. I go where I damn well please." I feel my heartbeat racing and not out of lust but anger. How dare he tell me no?

"I need you to shake your attitude and talk to me." This is the real Dylan. The mule-headed man that does things when he pleases and not a minute sooner. The humor in his eyes leaves me livid.

"We're good." I cross my arms over my chest.

"Most women would love to have this conversation with me. About a future beyond one night in my bed. Although I can promise, you'll love it." His brows wiggle.

"And that's my cue to leave."

"Fine." He loosens his grip and I push against his chest. I'm on my knees using the back of the couch for balance. I wiggle the fabric back over my breast and he licks his lips as if remembering. I hope he got a good taste because that will be the last one.

My inner voice, that clearly forgot our *no more Dylan* chant, is laughing at me. I'm committing to walking off and him begging me to return. I pull the hem of my dress slowly over my exposed bottom, I hear a groan from the couch. I toss my hair over my shoulder and look left and right searching for my shoes. I spot them beneath the coffee table.

"I love the way your lower lip quivers when you don't get your way." I freeze. I glance back and his eyes are changing again. Now is the time to leave while my dress is straight and he's still on the couch. I reach for my heels and before I know it, I'm in his arms.

"You lost your bargaining position the moment you let me taste you." His hands are lifting my dress and caressing my bottom.

"Let's not and say we did." I give him my best kiss-my-ass face and in a flash, his mouth is over mine. His tongue slips past my lips and dives deep. My legs are weak and his mouth is waging war against my determination to leave and not look back.

He licks down my neck and frees my breast again, a quiver runs down my spine as he nibbles and sucks his way lower. My dress is now on the floor. I'm naked except for my silver body necklace and he's kneeling at my feet.

"Are you going to behave?" His denim eyes challenge me to say anything but yes. He kisses my belly button. *Saying yes will change me forever.* But I feel powerless. "Yuki, say yes."

His finger trails down my lower stomach, my body—the traitor—is screaming *yes Dylan, yes Dylan, yes Dylan.* He stands and his hand is between my legs and my core is eager. To distract my mind, I reach for the bulge now resting against my stomach.

"Not yet baby. Let's get something clear." He

massages and probes until I'm wet and ready. "You are mine. Understand? No more Stewart."

Stewart was a willing date for social functions, never a serious relationship.

"And no more blondes?" I look up into his eyes. I trust him, my walls are tumbling faster than I can fathom and his eyes are pleading with me. It goes beyond words and the mounting desire between us. It goes to my heart.

"I accepted what you offered to have a piece of you. Waiting my turn, and I can't sit around waiting Yuki. I always knew you'd be my girl. And my heart knows having you will make everything in my life complete. Say yes Yuki and you won't regret it."

I'm fearless but at this moment with the plea in his eyes, I'm scared. Saying yes means opening myself up to fickle love.

My father never found a woman he didn't love. He loved my mother, he loved Momma, but not enough to commit to one woman.

Truth be told I trust Dylan but distrust love. Not when the one man in the world who should have loved me the most loved me the least. Remembering that made me a stronger woman. It taught me to trust the facts.

I drop my face not wanting him to see the doubts swimming in my soul.

"Don't shut me out, baby." He places a curled finger beneath my chin. "Tell me and I'll give it to you. But don't shut me out." Eyes filled with love wash over me, I nod fighting to remain present.

Can I do this, really? Love him the way he deserves. Give myself, not just my body, to him.

"You know I love you, right?" He smiles.

"Plainspoken as always." A calming truth enters my mind, the other men in my life didn't measure up because they were not him. Dylan is the standard.

"Don't let the past block our future." He continues.

But how can I keep the past in the past? It's as real as the air I'm breathing.

"Can we start with tonight?" I ask unsure I'm ready, yet I'm not willing to throw this opportunity away.

"I will do what it takes to prove that this," his finger touches my chest then his, "is it." That mule-headed determination is shining in his eyes and I should be worried. Concerned. But I'm not. All I can think is, *I'm Dylan's girl.*

"So this means I'm your girl?" I smile at the thought.

"No ma'am, you're my woman." He kisses me. Not the smoldering type but warm and filled with love. I can get used to this.

"What type of perks come with this position?"

He laughs and the mounting tension in my body eases. "Well, to start there's me, of course."

"Of course." I snicker.

"And I'm pretty sure I can top our couch session." For an instant, his eyes sharpen like a light switch turning on. His eyes cloud in a sexual haze.

"Oh really?"

"Yes, really." I accept the challenge in his voice brushing my hand over the front of his pants.

"Prove it."

CHAPTER 5

Dylan lifts me in his strong arms and carries me to the back. My stomach muscles clench and now we're standing in the doorway of what I assume is his bedroom. His assessing eyes are bold, studying me thoughtfully for a moment, my heart turns in response. *He's waiting.*

Powerless to resist, I answer the request swimming in the depths of his eyes. I kiss him, wanting to bask in his invisible warmth, his steadfast strength, and the declaration *you are mine*. And the aching returns.

"Yes, Dylan."

He stalks into the bedroom placing me on a king size bed, our eyes lock. He kisses up the length of my leg, to my knee, my thigh and pulls the knit fabric gathered at my waist down and tosses it across the room. I twist trying to tame the desire kindling as he and his eyes caress me from the foot of the bed.

A promising smile crosses his face, removing his shirt and his pants in a blink. He grabs me by the knees and pulls me to the edge of the bed, my legs straddling his body. His broad shoulders, defined abs, and…I smile at the gift aimed in my direction.

Dylan drops to his knees and I hear the sound of a package opening.

"Let me." I sit up and he passes the condom to me. I place it over his manhood and slowly roll it down to the base. He hisses, I glance up.

"Lay back." His deep voice simmers with unchecked passion and I like it. I follow his command, anxious for relief. He crawls on the bed his knees inside my thighs, spreading me open. I reach for him and guide him to my pulsating core and he pushes inside.

"Damn baby." We exhale and my body takes him in, filling me completely, our bodies joined as one. He thrusts deeper, his girth stretching me, my nails dig into his back.

"Dylan," I gasp. His body resting against mine, the light of the moon filling the room. He holds still and I rock my hips.

"Baby don't, you're so tight." A hungry sound escapes, I turn my head and see a bead of sweat trickle down the side of his face. Gripping his shoulders, I rock again, entranced by the connection between us.

"Please…."

Dylan pushes up on his hand, like before, except this time it's not his fingers filling me. Deep, steady strokes, our eyes locked, my body welcoming him deeper.

He murmurs words of love and I'm falling and falling fast in a tidal wave of Dylan. My walls grip him and I can't hold on much longer. His rhythm thrusting into my body in a passionate message. I'm hearing him loud and clear. I hold on tight as my eyes slide shut, every nerve, cell, and ligament at the mercy of him.

"Look at me." His words, wrapped in their labored breathing. I'm somewhere between torment and ecstasy.

"I can't," I confess.

He pulls out. Stunned, my eyes widen and his smile has a spark of eroticism. Dylan takes a quick breath then hammers in, I gasp for release then I shatter. Words of forever and a lifetime are flowing from him as overlapping waves of pleasure roll through me, I'm drowning as I scream his name for the world to hear.

His body jerks and with a roar of satisfaction, his

body goes limp. He drops to the mattress pulling me with him.

"I love you." His hot breath on my throat. *I love you too.*

I WAKE and I swear the little drummer boy is playing a solo inside my head. I roll over and my body is blocked by…*what the*—I force my eyes open peering under the black sheets, all I see is a bare chest. I look up and it's Dylan.

Dylan.

For the love of all that's—I glance down. Not even my body necklace survived. I'm naked in Dylan's bed. I squeeze my eyes shut trying to remember what happened last night.

Mexican food, tequila, *I love you.*

Did I say it back? I comb my hazy memory and I don't know. My neck snaps in his direction as he turns to the side causing the bed to bounce. He's always been a heavy sleeper, and he drank more tequila than me. I follow the lines in his chiseled back and see his naked backside. I reach out to—*No Yuki!*

I hold my throbbing head as the memories of making love a million ways until the sun peak through the room and now, I glance at the clock, two hours later I have to leave. I keep one eye on him and one eye on the edge of the bed. I scoot, pause. He's still breathing heavy.

Scoot, pause. He doesn't budge.

I slide off the edge of the bed sure to not move more than absolutely necessary. I drop on all fours. My head is protesting this entire escape plan. No more tequila for me. And I can't be here when he wakes.

I crawl across the room and find my dress. I glance over my shoulder searching for my panties. The time on the clock ignites a panic, he has a flight leaving for Ireland in three hours. I'm supposed to meet Asher at Mommas in an hour. I crawl as fast as my throbbing head will allow. I reach the bedroom door without waking him. I push to my feet and cover the space between the bedroom and the living room in haste holding my head in one hand and my dress in the other.

I catch a glimpse of myself in the mirror. The evidence of last night and this morning are bitten across my body. I put on my dress and his jacket. I shrug into it then snatch up my shoes and purse.

My heart is screaming *don't leave*. But my brain is counting all the ways this could end badly for me, for us. My body wants to climb back in bed and beg for a repeat. He loved me on every inch of his kingsized bed. He took me from the front the back, leaving me satisfied and wanting more until we dropped off to sleep.

I'm at the elevator pressing the down arrow, hearing…*Don't shut me out.*

I can't do this.

I push the button in rapid succession as if it will speed up the process. Waiting with my eyes fixed on the bedroom door. Then I remember my earrings, I touch my ears. I have a hoop in my right ear and a stud in my left. I see the box on the table.

Ding.

I hold my breath praying it doesn't wake him, running across the room grabbing the box before the elevator doors close. Inside I fold over gulping down the urge to release dinner right here and now. I lean against the cold steel wall to balance as the elevator finally reaches the first floor.

The doors open. I button his jacket around me, thankful the lobby is empty except for a lady with a service cart down the hall. I push my nose into the fold of my elbow smelling his cologne, my eyes mist as more memories surface from last night.

Was this how my father felt when he walked away from us? Slipping out undetected. Did his heart break for me? For mother? I shake off the thoughts. He has nothing to do with us.

Us.

I walk faster as Dylan's voice rings in my head, *you are mine.* I cross the lobby half naked, barefooted, and ashamed, aiming to put as much distance between Dylan and me as possible. I brush away the tears and stiffen my back. I stroll through the lobby pretending my heart will recover and somehow Dylan will forgive me, heading to the one place I need more than anything right now.

I head home.

CHAPTER 6

Is it possible to be whole yet incomplete? To stand at the doorway of the best possible outcome and it all crumbles due to fear.

I sit at a traffic light not able to fully process the last twelve hours. The light turns green, I grip the steering wheel driving through the empty streets heading to Momma's house.

What's wrong with me? Somehow in one night, I experienced heaven and now hell is raging in my chest. I managed to hurt a man I truly love. I beat the wheel with my closed fist. I'm crying and frustrated. My phone rings and I glance at the display.

Dylan.

I swallow hard, pressing the silence button my foot weighing heavy on the accelerator. I use the sleeve of his jacket to dry my face and his scent surrounds me with his denim eyes and declarations of love.

My heart is warring with itself and it's my fault. I pull into Momma's driveway. Asher pulls in behind me.

"Crap!" I look in the rearview mirror. I see his mouth moving, he must be on a call. Then I catch a glimpse of myself. I smooth my hair down, yank the jacket closed.

My foot touches the ground and I make a mad dash for the front door.

"Yuki..." he calls from behind me. I stop not turning around. He'll know what I did. "Good morning sis." He walks up beside me pulling me into a side hug. He glances down getting a real good look at me, his mouth falls open. "What are you wearing?"

"Good morning." I swallow hard, lifting my chin to meet his gaze. "Where are we going for breakfast?"

"Breakfast?"

I continue walking leaving him shocked near my car. I reach the porch and Momma opens the door. She gives me the once over and steps aside. I whisper, "Thank you."

"Mmmhum. We'll talk after you clean up."

I rush past, she'll handle Asher. I kiss her cheek and head for my bedroom. This house became my home twenty years ago. Momma took me in and later adopted me. The peace I find with her is unlike any other, except with Dylan. *I won't cry.*

I enter my childhood bedroom. It remains the same since high school. I spend the night with Momma a few times a month but today it is my refuge.

I shower and change into a pair of jeans and a t-shirt. I hear a soft tap at the door as I search the closet for shoes.

"Come in." I call out as I find some old Nike's. I put them on and step out to see Momma sitting on my bed, waiting.

"Grab the brush."

I grab it and a few ponytail holders sitting in front of her on the bed. I see her in the reflection of the mirror on my dresser. Our most significant conversations took place during hair time. Life, grades, conflicts, boys, all seemed to disappear like the tangles in my thick hair with the pass of a brush in Momma's hands.

"Asher's waiting," I remind her as she parts my hair with her hands using her fingers to separate my curls. She tosses half over my shoulder and I braid it loosely while she starts the detangling process.

"He'll survive." A flash of humor crosses her face.

I laugh. "Besides it seems both my babies are battling with their hearts today."

I drop my head and play with the pink ruffles on my bedspread. I feel the brush rake through my hair a few times. Smooth as silk. "How do you detangle my hair so fast?"

"Years of practice." She braids the section and adds an elastic band to the end to keep it from unraveling. She unbraids the other half and starts over.

"I slept with Dylan last night." I blurt out. Her hands stop, suspended in air, our eyes locking in the reflection of the mirror.

"Can't say I'm surprised." Now, I'm surprised.

"Why not?"

"That boy's been goo-goo eyed for you ever since he and Asher figured out girls were better than video games."

"Momma!" Her hearty laugh fills the room.

"It's true. I'm just glad he waited until you were good and grown." She continues working her way through my hair. "How do you feel about it?"

"About last night?" I'm watching her every move. She nods. "Confused."

"Why?"

I struggle to find the right words. I make high dollar presentations to billionaires persuading them to trust me with their brands. Nearly three billion dollars worth of contracts I've closed and I'm at a loss for words.

"This morning I remembered the last day I saw Dad with Mother." She looks away. "I was at the kitchen table working on a project for school and they were arguing as usual. And then peace settled over the room. I felt a shift."

I saw my five foot two Korean mother standing before my six-foot-tall father. They were the most striking couple like magnets either attracting or repelling.

"I later realized it was the day she learned about you and Asher," I remember looking up from my assignment, their love was so intense and volatile.

"What happened?"

"She confronted him. He didn't deny that you two were still married. Mother went crazy. Kicking, screaming, crying. He just stood there." Her mother collapsed on the couch her sobs filling the air. "That's when I knew I'd never see him again."

Momma finishes the last braid and pulls me to her. She kisses my forehead, wrapping a loving arm around me.

"She was on the couch yelling. Telling him to get out of her house. Never come back. He walked over to me and kissed my forehead and said, 'Love you, sweetie.' The next time I saw him, he was in a casket."

Momma's shirt is soaked with my tears. She knows the rest of my story. My father's death killed my mother, she died shortly after. But Momma saved me. Her and Asher found me right before my seventh birthday.

Her grip tightens, "Baby, we all manage our wounds in different ways. You erect a perfect, pristine steel wall. You're the princess in the ivory tower. Pretending to move beyond it all but you took your father's death the hardest. It was like you had something to prove."

I did.

"While your brother stands in front of anything and everything with a bulletproof vest, guarding his heart but not his life."

"What about you Momma?" I glance up.

"Me? Baby, I've learned to look at my wounds with gratitude." She nods her head and smiles. Her heart shines through her smile. "I was told I'd never have children. And not only did I have one. But the good Lord gave me two. *God is good to me.*" She holds me tight and raises her other hand to the sky.

"Cleo and his ways could have crushed me. But 20 years ago his restless spirit blessed me with you. My precious baby girl. A gift that I'd bear any wounds, tears, and heartaches to have."

My father married Momma before shipping out

in the Army. She remained in Texas while he traveled the world. He had women on almost every continent. And mother was the only one to follow him back to the United States after her parents disowned her. Asher and I are only a few weeks apart, I was born to my mother in Korea and him to Momma in the U.S. But father always loved Momma and it killed my mother.

"Is that what had you dragging in here this morning?" She chuckled.

"Mom!"

"Don't mom me. You came in with your bed hair and love bites all over you. I'm old but not *that* old."

"He told me he loved me and I left before he woke up this morning."

I wonder how he felt waking up in an empty bed? I glance in the mirror trying to discern her silence.

"Did he hurt you?" Her face is unreadable.

"No."

"Do you not return his feelings?"

I can't look in her eyes. Dylan is like another child to her and I'm sure it's hard to see either of us hurting.

"All I see is my mother's face and I feel my father's, cold heart. I can't love him like this." For the first time I feel unworthy, like my baggage is too heavy.

"And you don't think he knows that? That boy knows you better than any of us. He accepts you as you are and at some point, you have to do the same." She shows no signs of letting up.

"I can't hide with him." I confess.

"And that's a bad thing? Baby look at me." She grips my shoulders and we're face to face. "Every relationship is different. You are not your parents. If you don't love Dylan, fine. But don't run from love. You have too much of it to give."

"Thank you," I whisper.

"Yuki Smith loving you is an absolute joy. I couldn't ask for more. The good Lord would deem me selfish and ungrateful." She chuckles at her own joke, I love this woman.

"What about you Momma? Don't you want to be in love again."

"My life's full." Her sentiments echo my own. Then she falls silent again. "How about we make a Smith Pact?"

Smith Pacts are written in stone. Unbreakable. It was how she taught us to keep our promises to each other and ourselves. I sit up, knowing not to take it lightly.

"We will," Momma reaches for my hands, "open our hearts to love."

I nod in agreement and hug her. "Thank you, Momma."

"You're welcome, my love. Now, let me go see what's eating your brother." She kisses my forehead then leaves the room.

I gather Dylan's jacket and head to the living room to check on Asher. Then I'll call Dylan.

CHAPTER 7

"Is Jazz ready for her little trip? I'm taking you up on your offer and joining her." I need a vacation.

Asher and I took Momma to breakfast and told her the good news about Smith & Jameson. My talk with Momma left me feeling refreshed except for the minor task of calling Dylan. Thankfully I have his number at the hotel in Dublin. I'm watching the clock to give him time to land and get settled in.

"Actually I need to ask you for a favor?"

"What is it?" Asher is staring at me as if he's about to drop a bomb.

"I need you to fly to Ireland in my place." His eyes are avoiding mine. "I'll cover your ticket, the accommodations—"

"What happened?"

"You'll love the place. We booked a private tour to view the Blarney Castle and—"

"Asher—"

"...and there's a two day Beer and Bike tour visiting several breweries. You'll love that too." He's rambling.

"Asher!"

He faltered, shocked. "I messed up bad."

"Don't worry we'll fix it." I say the words but his face has me concerned.

"Not even my lucky charm can fix this one." He runs his hand over his face. "Jazz and I had a huge fallout and I gave her a hall pass."

"*You did what?*"

"I gave her—"

"I heard you. What were you thinking giving your *wife* permission to do what and whoever she wants?"

"I wasn't. And I didn't think she'd actually believe me." He's pacing the length of the living room. I sit back on the couch sending up a silent prayer for my brother and Jazz. This has got to be the craziest weekend ever.

I hold up my hands to stop the pacing, he's making me dizzy. "What happened?"

"I found out she stopped taking her birth control because she wants a baby." I gasp out of reflex. "Tell me about it. So I'm pissed. She's going on and on about me not being there for her. That I'm consumed with Smith & Jameson. And how she wants out." He stops. It's like fumes are rising from his head.

"Calm down."

"I'm calm," he barks.

I roll my eyes and he drops to the couch.

"How did that conversation lead to a hall pass?" I can't see Jazz actually doing it. Something else is going on.

"She said something like 'I need space' and next thing I know I say 'Do whatever you want but divorce is not an option.'"

"Asher please tell me you didn't." I walk over and sit next to him. He's folded over. "What are you going to do?" Romantic woes are rabid in the Smith family today.

"I'm not begging her to stay. I'm a good husband. I don't cheat. I take care of her. I'm more of a man than our father ever was." His last statement pierces my heart and I think about the pact I made with Momma. "This is the Twilight Zone."

"Tell me about it. I slept with Dylan last night."

"You what?" He glances up. "If this is some sort of reverse psychology, I can't take no more surprises."

"I did and I love him. I have for a long time now."

"Of course you love him, we know that. But are you in love with him?"

I nod. And his eyes move over me at lightning speed, "What happened?"

"I left before he woke up."

"That's probably why he called me this morning."

My body stiffens. "Did you talk with him?"

"No, I was too busy losing my wife." The agony in his voice is palpable.

"What are you going to do?"

"Besides apologize and hope I don't have to kill a dude for touching my wife?" He cracks his knuckles.

I've never seen Asher like this. The seriousness in his face is scary. But I don't see Jazz trying to sleep with another guy or skipping out on her birth control. She must be trying to get his attention. Now it's time I do the same.

"Brother, I have an idea to repair our relationships."

THE SMITH PACT is in full effect as I exit the terminal in Dublin Ireland. Asher headed to Cancun and I'm pulling my carry-on through the modern airport. We landed early giving me time to grab a coffee and consider how I'm going to apologize.

I call Momma and she lets me know Asher made it safely too. I exhale, nervous energy assaults me as I head to the exit to look for my driver. I'm officially on my own risking it all hoping Dylan hears me out.

"Hello, I'm Yuki Smith." I see a man in a black suit holding a sign with my name on it.

"Welcome to Dublin Ireland." His smile lights up the room and I feel an adventure in my future.

"Thank you." He reaches for my bag and we make our way to the car. "I am thrilled and exhausted."

He laughs and opens the door for me. We ride into the center of town where a sizeable pin-like structure points to the sky appearing to fit right in yet almost odd. "What is that?"

"You are looking at the Spire of Dublin. You should walk over and see it later tonight."

"What else would you recommend?"

"There are several parks within walking distance, free museums, and the Dublin castle. If you're looking for tourist type places, there's Temple Bar." He slows down turning into the hotel. He walks around and lets me out. "Temple Bar is not like a traditional American bar. It is more like an area of bars together with music and of course plenty of beer."

He rolls my bag to the sidewalk as a doorman

steps forward. I turn towards him to give a tip. "No thank you. It was covered with your reservation."

I smile. "Thank you again. Is there anywhere else you'd suggest?"

"How long are you here?"

"A little under a week. I have plans for Guinness tomorrow and Blarney Castle later in the week."

"Those are great choices. Keep your eyes open for great authentic Irish crafts and don't forget the ale." We laugh. "Many of these locations are within walking distance or a quick bus. But you'd miss a treat if you don't visit the Cliffs of Moher." I was so anxious about seeing Dylan again that I didn't do much research. "What's your name again?"

"Call me Art."

"Art thank you again. Take care."

I enter the hotel ready for my next big challenge. Thankfully, Asher handled everything. Minutes later I enter the double bed suite, I shower and set my timer for one hour. Traveling fourteen hours with a layover knocked the wind out of me. Sleeping before connecting with Dylan ensures I'm focused and have my wits about me. Turning down the covers, I climb into the plush bed and fall asleep as soon as my head hits the pillow.

〜

"Hey, Siri what time is it?" The room is pitch black.

"It's 8:27 PM. Good evening, Yuki."

I pop up rested, I must have hit the snooze button a million times. I toss back the covers and swing my feet over the side of the bed. I hear a sharp intake and look up to see someone in the chair across the room.

"Who are you?" I reach for the phone.

"What are you doing here? And where are your clothes?"

CHAPTER 8

I'm going to kill Asher. It'll be slow and painful. Pliers and a screwdriver. No one will suspect it, I wouldn't risk Jazz's chance to get his life insurance policy—I clearly watch too many movies. I reach for the blanket.

"Leave it."

I stare at his silhouette aware of the occupant in the chair and what he's thinking. He's pissed. What do I plan to do about it? I push the covers back as he requested. The long trip gave me time to decide if this is what I want and I do. Now to get him to see it.

I'm opening my heart to love.

I stand as naked as the day I was born with the addition of my diamond studs. I walk to the mini bar thankful for every yoga class and run. My abs are tight, butt is high and round but Dylan is a leg man —and I got legs for days.

I bend slowly at the waist with my tush in the air. I grab a bottle of water turning my head in his direction. The soft light peaking around the perimeter of the drapes ensures he gets an eyeful.

"Would you like some?" I stand, cracking the seal on the bottle, facing him taking a long drink. This is the deal of all deals.

My talk with Momma lessened the ache of the hurt from my past, maybe one day the good days will overshadow the bad. But at this moment I thank my parents because I hit the genetic lottery. I have my father's height and full lips, my mother's alluring eyes, and my caramel skin is a perfect blend of both. With the addition of Momma's heart and courage, which I'll need to make Dylan love me again.

I walk in his direction.

"Stop." His hoarse whisper breaks the silence.

My heart is lodged in my throat. I can play up the sexuality, tease him until he folds, or tell him the truth. I choose the latter, starting with his question, "I came here to get you back."

"Why so you can leave in the middle of the night?"

"No, I—"

"So you can ignore all of my calls?"

"Dylan, I—"

"Yuki, you are not going to walk all over me like those other dudes. You don't want what I have to offer, fine. But no games."

"I'm not playing—"

He's on his feet. The heat off his body reaching out to me across the room. I step towards him.

"Don't." His hands up like two large stop signs. "You played me."

"But you said, I'm yours."

"Don't use my words against me." He growls.

I take another step. "Dylan, I'm sorry. You opened up to me and I was overwhelmed. I didn't know how to give you what you deserve. So I—"

"Left." The finality in his voice cuts like a rusty knife.

I'm losing him. I step back and hear Momma's voice, *don't run from love.* I step forward.

"Before I came to live with Momma and Asher I lived with my parents. My father, Cleo Smith, was career military and an officer in the Army. He was stationed in Korea when he met my 18-year-old mother, Sun-young Lee."

I sit on the end of the bed. "He was tall, handsome, and worldly. She was a petite beauty sheltered by her parents. They moved fast, so fast that when it was time for him to return to the States she found out she was pregnant. He left anyway and all seemed well in her world until her parents saw her little black baby girl with thick curly hair."

"You?"

I nod. My heart considers what it must have been like for my mother to be a young girl facing her parents alone with a baby, let alone a black baby. Her bundle of joy destroyed her relationship with her parents forever.

"They disowned her. Pregnancy before marriage was bad enough but by a black man... They gave her an ultimatum, give me up for adoption or move out. She moved out and they cut her out of their lives completely leaving her with no choice but to reach out to my father. And he sent for her."

I've never told anyone this story. I climb beneath the covers as the air conditioner turns on.

"So there she was with a newborn, speaking little English and he moves her to Texas before being deployed again. And for years we lived in a bubble. Just the two of us. He'd pop in here and there between tours. It wasn't until years later I learned he had another family."

"Asher and Momma."

"Yep and it was the day of the funeral." A freak accident took his life. I brush the tears away and for the first time, the ache of my father's betrayal doesn't carry the same sting. "I learned he was married to his high school sweetheart. They had a son. And nowhere was I mentioned in his obituary."

"Did they know?"

"No." I shake my head.

"Were there others?"

"Not that we know of." I fluff a pillow and lean it against the headboard and Dylan sits beside me. "Learning about Momma Smith broke my mother's heart. Dad dying signed her death certificate. The light left her eyes, she was like the living dead. I did everything I could to make her happy but it seemed like her happiness died with him."

"I'm sorry baby." He wraps an arm around me.

"By the time I was six, I'd buried my father and my mother and that's when Momma found me." I smile as I realize how blessed I am. "She kept me from going to the foster care system. She took me in loving me like her own. Asher did the same. And I thought it was enough until I crawled out of your bedroom."

I thought I wanted space but the last couple days taught me all I want is him. With him, I feel safe and adored. *He's worth it.*

They say confession is good for the soul, I'd agree minus my racing heart and the uncertainty of his response. The darkness masks his face, his arm tightens around me, encouraging me to continue. "I've loved you for as long as I can remember but the thought of actually having you scared me. I've never seen love work. Even my brother and Jazz, they are fighting to save their marriage and I couldn't wrap my brain around having you only to lose you."

"You'd never lose me, baby." He kisses me softly on the lips.

"What about now? Did I lose you? Do you still love me?" I turn towards him hopeful, determined to prove that we belong together.

"Always."

I exhale breathing freely for the first time since leaving his bed.

"Can we please give this a try?" I cup his face in my hands rubbing a thumb over his lips. "Please Dylan." I kiss him. Again, and again. I straddle his body. "I won't shut you out again."

I kiss his neck.

"I know that I can't control you." I giggle.

"Are you laughing at me?" The humor in his voice lets me know I'm winning.

"No sir." I plan to lay it on thick. "I'd never laugh at you."

"Now I know you're lying."

Next thing I know I'm on my back. His face is hovering over mine and I feel his peace all around me.

The heat of his thighs on the outside of mine, his familiar scent surrounding me. This is the part of my life that money and deals can't satisfy. True peace.

"Dylan."

"Yes, baby."

"Make love to me."

He doesn't hesitate as his mouth finds mine in a heartbeat, his tongue exploring the depths of my mouth filling me with a new happiness. I reach for the hem of his shirt, he releases my mouth as I pull it over his head. I kiss his chest reaching between my legs for the button on his jeans.

Dylan grabs my hands pinning them above my head.

"That is so unfair." I whine between kisses.

"Are you going to fight me about everything?"

I thought about it. "Only when you're wrong."

His robust laughter fills the room and my heart. "I think I have a way to quiet that sassy mouth."

"Prove it."

"Don't mind if I do."

He stands crossing the room, moving around in the dark. I hear a zipper, the rustle of plastic, and he's back climbing into the bed beside me. My heart pounds at his nearness, anticipating the fill of him inside me. He covers my body with his, I shiver and press myself against him. Skin to skin the sweetness of his breath feathers across my face, I turn my mouth seeking his.

We kiss. I lift from the bed trying to drink him in as his mouth commands and I willingly obey. He pulls away covering the terrain of my body with precision, sucking my neck, nibbling on my shoulder and covering my breast with his warm mouth, like a starved man as he massages the other.

His actions are loud and clear as he stakes his claim over my body. Every touch of his hands feels like a promise. And I know I made the right decision of following him, with him is where I belong.

I cup his firm butt in my hands pulling him closer as an ache, that only he can satisfy, mounts. I rock my hips against him wanting him now. Impatience leads my hand exploring beneath the covers.

"Not yet love."

"Dylan...." His hands hold my waist and in a single thrust, he fills me. Every inch. The air leaves my lungs. He pulls out and plunges in again. "Ahhh...."

"No...more...running." I arch my hips meeting him stroke for stroke, the headboard slamming the wall, our tattered breathing fills the air. "Say it Yuki or I'll pull out."

"Don't!" My walls start to quiver and I won't last

much longer. This is unlike anything I've ever experienced with any man. I tell him so.

"Say it!" His voice commands thick with passion.

"No more running." The words tumble out. He could ask me to run across the Brooklyn bridge for cheesecake and I'd ask how many slices. I'm clawing his sweat covered back begging him to not stop.

"You are mine." His energy is rushing through my body, pushing out my doubts and he's right, I'm his.

"I'm yours." He slips an arm beneath my knee opening me wider and he drives deeper before his growl fills the room drowning out my cry of ecstasy.

He kisses me tenderly. "I love you Yuki."

"I love you too."

THE CLOCK SAYS it's a little after seven in the morning and I can't sleep. I am cuddled next to Dylan in a full sized bed and I've never been happier. I roll over and snuggle against his chest.

"Baby we have to be in the lobby in an hour." He sounds exhausted.

"Why?" I want to stay in bed and make love to him all day. We have time to make up for.

"I scheduled a tour guide for the day to visit Blarney Castle."

My head pops up, "To kiss Blarney's Stone?"

"If you'd like, I have no plans on kissing a rock that millions of people have kissed. But if that's what floats your boat." He chuckles. "We'll see the old castles, the countryside, visit a few breweries, the works."

"Yay. Mind if I use the bathroom first."

"Not at all." I hop up and run towards the bathroom. I back peddle and kiss him nice and slow. "Good morning to you too."

I laugh slipping into the bathroom. My life feels perfect. Super perfect. Better than perfect. I had this week scheduled off for my birthday but I need to check my emails before we head out. And to think I'll be in Dublin for my 27th birthday.

"Thank you, Momma," I squeal under the hot running water. She talked some sense into me.

"Time's ticking baby," Dylan yells through the door.

"I'm coming," I yell back. I check my reflection and decide, forget it. I'll go with no makeup. I step out, "It's all yours." He smacks my bare bottom and enters in on my heels.

I dress in jeans and a shirt with sneakers. I search my bag for a hat then I plait my hair in a single braid —my Lara Croft style. Pleased with the outcome, I move to the little kitchen area putting on a pot of coffee, adding a little gloss to my lips while I wait.

Dylan walks out of the bathroom, stopping with his arms full of clothes. "You look beautiful."

I search his eyes for humor and see none. "And no, I'm not joking, I never understood why you wear all that makeup in the first place." He kisses me then moves on to his luggage on the other bed.

Ten minutes after a cup of coffee we are headed to the elevator hand in hand. Dublin here we come.

CHAPTER 9

Gerald, the tour guide is giving us the rundown. He opens a map and spreads it across the hood. "Now here we are here," he turns the map and says we're at the bottom. "Blarney Castle is here."

"What about Cliffs of Moher?" I recall from speaking with Art yesterday.

"Beautiful spot," he says, "it is over here." His fingers are pointing to locations in opposite directions.

"Is it possible to see both today?" Dylan asks.

Gerald shrugs. "Anything is possible."

"What would you recommend?" Dylan says as the old man flattens his hands on the map to keep it from blowing away.

"I'd make it an overnight trip. It will give us a leisurely pace. We can stop at various locations between our destinations. But I need to verify that I don't have a tour booked tomorrow. If not, I'd love to give you a world class tour of my country."

"That cool with you Yuki?"

"Yes." I smile eager to get rolling.

"We'd love that too. How long will it take for you to confirm everything?" Dylan turns helping Gerald fuss with folding the map closed.

"Give me an hour. Actually, have you had breakfast?"

"No." Dylan says reaching for me.

"I'll take you over to spot to get a traditional Irish breakfast and while you eat, I'll talk with the office."

"Work in time for us to pack a bag and you got yourself a deal." They shake hands and we hop into the car.

Riding through town Gerald points out historical buildings and parks. "Back in that area is the Temple Bar area."

"Is Impose Brew in Temple Bar too?" Dylan looks to the right of the car.

"Yes." Gerald glances in the rearview mirror at us. "You have Dubh Linn Gardens, Dublin Castle, and Saint Stephens Green. Finally, many of our guests love visiting Trinity College to see the Book of Kells, which is a famous medieval manuscript of the Gospels of Jesus Christ."

"I think I need to plan a longer stay next time," I whisper to Dylan and he agrees.

In record time, we are eating breakfast of eggs, sausage, a ham-like meat, tomatoes, toast and black pudding. Gerald confirms his schedule and after stopping by the hotel to pack we are on the road heading to Blarney Castle.

The adventure ahead has me jumping out of my skin.

Traffic moves slowly for a while then the highway opens up. With Gerald behind the wheel, I lean into Dylan watching the clouds. I am in a car riding through Ireland with Dylan Jameson. Crazy.

"Has this sunk in yet? I look up and he scratches my scalp pulling his eyes away from his iPad.

"What's that baby?"

"You and I. Like official."

"When you say it like that, I guess so. But I always knew it would happen, it was all a matter of when." He kisses me with a smack then goes back to reading.

"How could you be so sure?" This was the funny part of love that's over my head. I don't doubt my love for him. It just is. But the words elude me.

"How can you not?" He lowers his iPad to his lap and I sit up facing him. "We are devoted to our families. High achievers. Career driven but not obsessed.

We balance each other. You are a bull in the China shop, I'm more, why argue, I'll buy you out?"

I laugh. "And I'm the bull?"

His forehead wrinkles as if in thought. "Okay, so I'm a bull too. I guess as I think about it those are important qualities. I know part of my love is rooted in who you were and getting to know the woman now makes it feel like a forever love." He wraps his hand around my neck and pulls me closer. "We're made for each other and for me, this is the one thing that doesn't have to make sense to anyone but you."

His confidence in me is astounding.

"It makes sense." I smile knowing for sure this man is it for me. Nothing about my legs or my accomplishments. He truly loves me, for me.

"I see us old and gray with grandkids, traveling the world, doing everything or nothing. As long as I can do it with you." He turns back to read and glances back over at me. "What changed your mind?

"Momma."

"Momma?"

"Yes, she helped me see that I am the sum of my parents but her too. And she is heart and courage and love." I search for another word. "And resilient." I lay back against his chest. "And we made a pact."

"A Smith Pact? Oh goodness." He laughs, never taking things or himself too seriously.

"Hush. We promised to open our hearts to love."

"And just like that, you board a plane to Ireland?"

"No, just like that I decided to tell you how I really feel. To love you and accept your love in return. So I boarded the plane for you."

"I like the sound of that."

"No more than I, I promise you."

We kiss. Not the first kiss, not the last. But it feels like crazy glue connecting my heart to his. "Now before I jump your bones in the back seat tell me about Impose Brew."

"Honey, don't tempt me." I elbow him and lean back snuggling into his side. He turns his iPad back on and passes it to me. "Impose Brew is the reason I'm here. It's the last brewery I want to complete our lineup. I'm hoping Asher sending his good luck charm will make this deal happen."

"Oh, the pressure." He chuckles and I feel lucky. How can I not with Dylan by my side? I turn my focus to reading through the website. Any help I give Dylan helps my brother, and they are the most important men in my life. I start at the About Us page. They are 100% Irish owned offering seasonal and one-off brews. "Impressive."

"Tell me what you see. I trust your eye and brains." He kisses my forehead and I scan the page as if this was a potential client. I click through the pages and visit each of their social media pages. I'd change their verbiage and website color scheme but all-in-all they are an attractive brand.

"I like the branding, the label is unique, catchy yet not a cliche. It reads having a good time, Gen X, which should definitely blend with S&J."

"S&J?"

"Yes, I've meant to talk with you guys. Smith & Jameson sounds lush, high end. Which is accurate. But you should have niche events under S&J. Sleek, fresh, young vibes targeting young professionals. They have more discretionary income and more time to hang out in the garden eating international truck food."

He nods. "I like that. What else do you see with Impose? They've declined every offer. I need to find an edge to get the owner to see me before we leave. I figure doing it in person will make my offer more appealing."

"I'm sure it will help. They have the food industry buzz words too. Natural ingredients. Unique and bold flavors. Authentic." Not bad for a family-owned business. I read through some of the reviews. "Did they give you a reason for declining?"

"They all boil down to wanting to keep the company a family operation."

"Do you have your last offer on here?" I hold up the iPad.

"I should have it in the cloud. Let me find it."

I sit up to give him use of both hands. Thinking about offers, I open my mail app and scroll through my emails. "Oh no." My stomach drops.

"What?" He glances over.

"I have an email from Jack." I close my eyes and say a quick prayer. I don't expect an offer by email. But why else would he email me knowing I'm on vacation?

"Want me to open it?"

"Would you?" He reaches for my phone and I shake off the nervous energy. *I control my destiny.* I've done the work. The promotion is mine. He looks over his shoulder offering a supportive squeeze on my thigh. "I'm ready."

"Yuki, you and Eric have made the selection process the hardest we've experienced since opening the doors of BrandShare. Congratulations on being a standout VP and for the way you represent our brand. To aid in making our selection, I'm running an ad hoc competition between you and Eric. The winner will be our next partner."

"Competition?" I shout. Gerald's eyes are bouncing between the road and the rearview mirror. Apparently, he's getting a kick out of this too.

"Calm down baby." He reaches over, lacing his fingers with mine. "Ready?"

I nod, not trusting myself to speak.

"The person to close the highest, new account by July 7th will be our new partner."

"Highest, new, July 7th." I say the words aloud to cement them in my mind.

"Do they know that's your birthday?"

"And technically while I'm out on vacation." I chew my lip and scan my mind for clients. New clients mean they can be past clients. Last count, I have the highest gross for new business in the firm outside the partners. But I never underestimate my competition.

"I can make some calls." His eyes are trained on me.

Dylan works purely because it's what he enjoys. He could never work another day in his life and still be abundantly wealthy. His parents invested in a tech start-up in Texas and pulled out before things bottomed out. Then they move on to Silicon Valley. S&J is his first solo venture in entrepreneurship. It's a passion project for him and Asher, neither are worried about turning a profit. Sound business is what fuels them and that is where we are alike.

"No, I'll figure it out."

"I'll let it go under one condition."

"And that is?"

"You let me know if there is any way I can help. What's mine is yours."

"I got it."

"I'm serious. I'll call Jack, Eric and whoever else is needed." A stubborn crease deepened between his brows.

"Dylan! This is not my first rodeo, or apparent setup." I whisper the last of the sentence. I don't need Dylan running to my rescue. *I'm my own rescue.* I sit back and a lightbulb the size of Texas turns on. I lean close to the driver's seat. "Excuse me, yesterday my driver told me about an area that has authentic Irish crafts."

Gerald looks over his shoulder, seemingly shocked to see my head between the seats. "There are several areas you can visit. There's Drury Street. One my wife enjoys is Irish Design."

"What's the difference?"

"Drury is more classics and Irish Design is a modern take on the classics. Equally as beautiful. They have soaps, clothes, jewelry. You can get carried away and spend your entire savings." He smiles, as ideas collide in my head. "And if you love jewelry there is Irish Celtic jewelry, candlestick holders, the options are endless."

"Thank you." I sit back. That's all I need.

Dylan's large hands take my face and he kisses me with such passion that it shocks me.

"What was *that* for?" His smile is as intimate as the kiss, a mind-tingling shiver of wanting runs through me.

"Your mind makes me want to," he leans closer brushing his lips near my ear, "take you right here and now." I look in the rearview mirror. Yep, we have an audience. Dylan makes me feel like I can do anything and he'll love me for it.

"Next time," I promise. His smile deepens into laughter. "Now where is that proposal?"

"Don't worry about Impose Brew."

"Hand it over." His eyes widen and he hands over the iPad. I read the proposal and immediately notice several key elements missing. "Email this to me."

Dylan opens his mouth as if to object when the car stops. I glance out the window.

"Welcome to Blarney Castle."

CHAPTER 10

Dylan jumps out and reaches for my hand. We both turn towards the castle, I immediately turn my phone off. This is the type of moment you have to give your full attention.

"The castle dates back to the late 1400s. It's technically the third castle built here and these are the original remains." Gerald closes his door and stands beside Dylan. "Inside you can tour the castle, gardens, the Blarney Stone. It can take thirty to forty-five minutes or hours. My time is yours."

"Knowing this one," Dylan looks over at me, "we'll need a couple hours."

"Sure. I can accompany you inside."

"I think we have it under control. I have your number if anything changes. Should I call when we're ready?"

"No, I'll be here with a book." Gerald smiles and climbs back in the car.

"Ready?" I'm ready to get inside. My research this morning did this place no justice.

"Lead the way babe." I drag him along pushing aside Impose Brew and BrandShare.

Dylan buys our tickets and we pass through the gift shop. The area before us is green and full of colorful flowers. We both have to duck to keep the trees from whacking us.

Then the sidewalk transforms into a gravel path, surrounded by plush, thick grass and aged stone. The Blarney River is our companion as we inch our way through the magnificent gardens.

"The grounds are impeccable."

"And peaceful." He kisses me as if he can't help it and I kiss him back. We continue our slow tour talking about everything but work. Taking every left and right available exploring every inch until we enter the castle.

The stone is an ashen gray covered in moss. I look up and the roof is exposed. Dylan notices a sign affixed to the wall. We are standing in the Family Room and it tells of the windows and fireplaces to liven up the space.

"That's pretty cool." I take his outreached hand entering the castle. We move from room to room.

They have updated the stairs but the beauty of the ruins are left intact. The inner area has high ceilings that are a mixture of smooth and rough textures, aged and decaying, is part of its authenticity.

Next, we climb a narrow stairway following the signs to the stone. The tight squeeze leads us to the top of the tower. I step out with Dylan's assistance and all I see is treetops, fluffy white clouds, and endless sky.

He pulls me to him. "This puts life into perspective."

"It does." I wrap my arms around his waist. This brush with the beauty of the past fortifies my resolve to excel in the challenge posed by Jake and create a full life outside of work. I glance up. "I kind of like being your woman."

"Well, I am a catch." He winks barely holding back his smile.

I laugh and it reaches the depths of my soul echoing off the ancient castle. Heads turn in my direction and I could care less.

"Watch it buddy or I'll throw you back out to the sea. Come on, I'm ready to kiss the stone."

I reach for the handrail and Dylan places a protective hand around my waist guiding me forward to kiss the stone. The legend says if you kiss it you'll have the gift of gab to charm people. Sounds a little like luck to me. I stand in line waiting my turn to seal the deal with my destiny. To find a new client, help S&J get Impose Brew as a vendor, and have a future full of success, happiness, and yes, *more Dylan*.

"You ready?" The worker is moving the line along.

I nod. It's my turn to hang 90 feet above the ground to kiss an ancient stone.

"Hold the bars and tilt your head to the bottom."

I follow his instructions lowering down, gripping the rusty bars tight and I kiss the stone with hope dancing in my belly.

THE REST of our excursions went by in the blink of an eye. The Cliff of Moher turned me into a lover of all things Ireland. We cross the countryside heading back to Dublin with only three days left before returning to Texas.

"Thank you for sharing this trip with me," Dylan whispers near my ear.

"Thank you for having me since I sort of invited myself." His laugh ripples through his chest against my back. I fall asleep with him promising to wake me once we arrive in Dublin, I close my eyes ready to take on my hectic life.

I WAKE in the middle of the night with a plan. I look over and Dylan is knocked out. I slide out of the bed quietly. The last time I left his bed I was frightened by the thought of love. This time I'm leaving to help S&J get Impose Brew.

I tiptoe to the small office and turn on my computer. I put on coffee and get to work. I rewrite their proposal. Impose Brew wanted to remain family owned and partnering with S&J could extend their family. S&J is a family owned company that supports other lesser known brands. This would expand their market while adding to their bottom line.

"Brilliant." I sip the hot coffee and type like a mad woman thankful my man sleeps like a log. I pull the facts and figures from the original proposal, a few calculated predictions, and some graphics of their unique labels. The S&J logo adds the finishing touch.

Pleased, I stretch and glance at the clock. It's only eleven o'clock. Impose Brew *is* a bar, what bar closes before midnight? None that I can think of. I toy with the idea of waking Dylan. What if the owner isn't there or declines my request?

I'll go and return before he knows I'm gone. And *when* the owner agrees, I'll call and wake him from his peaceful slumber. Satisfied with my plan I tiptoe across the room, grabbing some clothes and my makeup bag. In full ball buster mode, twenty minutes later, I'm in Temple Bar.

"I'll wait here for you."

"Thanks, Art, I'll be right back." I'm glad I'm not alone. I enter the bar and its crowded from wall to wall. It's a multilevel structure with bookcases lining the walls and self-serve taps at the tables. I cross the room, heads turn.

As a younger woman, I hated looking different. From the slant in my eyes to the hue of my skin, I know my uniqueness opens doors. All I need is a crack, from there I will kick the door down until I reach my destination. Hopefully kissing the Barney Stone actually works tonight because I'm strolling to the bar and I'm not taking no for an answer.

I ORDER a beer and listen to the chatter at the bar. I see a man interacting with the bartender and the waiters. He opens a door and disappears.

"What can I get for you?" I return his smile.

"Five minutes with him," I point towards the closed door, "and a mug of your best ale." I put a tip on the sticky bar and his eyes widen.

"I'll see what I can do." He places a mug in front of me and pockets the money.

I take a drink of the cold beer, stopping to stare at the glass with appreciation. The flavor is robust, silky on the tongue with a hint of fruitiness. *Damn*. Not only are they positioned in the market but this is what my guys need.

"Good evening beautiful."

CHAPTER 11

Awareness crawls up my spine at the edge in his voice. "Taste this."

I face Dylan with an outreached mug, his denim eyes shooting daggers. I plead with my eyes for him to take the mug.

"I was told you want to see me." I swallow the frog in my throat and place the beer on the bar, spinning on the stool. Straightening my back, ready to bless him with my gift of gab. "Yes. I traveled all the way from Texas to taste your beer and it did not disappoint."

"Right this way."

I stand and turn for a second to see Dylan. I place a hand on his forearm for the briefest second and his muscle tenses. *Stay…please,* I whisper praying he can hear me over the music. I plaster on my best smile and stroll to the office following the owner. The proposal will benefit Impose Brew and Smith & Jameson Beer Garden.

As I wrote the words, I experienced a rush of adrenaline that I haven't felt in years. This is what I'm missing, the heart. And I have the best incentive to make this work. I'm doing it for my brother and my man.

Luck don't fail me now.

CHAPTER 12

I sit in the offered chair praying Dylan waits for me. I turn to face the man behind the desk and notice a sign over his shoulder. "May you be touched by a bit of Irish luck."

I control my destiny. But I don't want it without Dylan. "Can you excuse me for one moment?"

"Make it quick."

I rush out of the office and Dylan is sitting on my empty barstool and he's finishing my beer. He shoots a penetrating look my way, I cover the distance in an instant.

"I can't do—"

"He's ready to meet with us about Smith & Jameson." An icy fear twists around my heart.

"Smith & Jameson?" His voice rises in surprise.

"I have less than a minute to complete my presentation. Will you please join me?"

"Let's go." He stands, confusion etched on his handsome face.

I walk back to the office needing a touch of the Irish luck. I push down the anxious feeling that I'm going to lose Dylan and focus on Impose Brew signing this contract.

We enter and Dylan holds out a chair for me and takes the other.

"I'm Yuki Smith." I glance over my shoulder.

"And I'm Dylan Jameson."

"Bradan. Nice to meet you both. I'm surprised to see you here. *Tonight.*"

I laugh. "I'm sure. We crossed the Atlantic to sit with you."

"I'm impressed."

"Not more than we are," Dylan says. And Bradan smiles inclining his head for me to proceed with my presentation.

"May I?" I pull a jump drive from my clutch.

"Sure." He moves his chair to the side and I launch into my presentation. I plan to give the whole spill in ten minutes but his questions drag it out to thirty.

"Can I get either of you an ale?"

"Yes, I'll have another Sweet Bliss."

"I'll take your bestseller," Dylan requests.

Bradan leaves the office heading to the bar. I turn to Dylan, I have two minutes max to beg his forgiveness, again.

"When did you do all of this?" There is a suspicious line at the corners of his mouth.

"This morning." His serious expression forces me into gab mode. "I know I left but I didn't want you to be disappointed if Bradan declined my meeting request. But I came with Art and I planned to call you as soon as I got the appointment."

"So you represent Smith & Jameson now?" He clenches his mouth tighter. "Or is this about your promotion to partner?"

"That's what you think this is?" I'm floored, he thinks I'm here for BrandShare.

Bradan returns with our beers. He appears eager to continue. I take a drink of my beer and dive into the numbers. He whistles.

"Your brand is about family but think of the legacy you'll build if you strategically align your brand with ours. You don't lose control or equity in your business. And you'll partner with other family-owned businesses."

"Family owned?"

"Yes, my brother and I are partners along with Dylan…." I didn't know what to call him. My friend.

My boyfriend. My twin's best friend. I glance over hoping for help but my mention of being a partner must have him shocked.

An hour later we have a signed contract, Dylan promises to submit the payment for the first order on Monday once we return to Texas.

"I look forward to working with Smith & Jameson," Bradan says shaking our hands.

"And we can't wait to share Impose Brew with the States."

ART IS outside waiting for me. He drives us back to the hotel. Dylan hasn't said a word since we left Impose Brew. I comb my brain for the right words to say as we walk back to our room. He pushes the door open and I step inside turning to face him.

"I'm sorry."

His mouth covers mine and I exhale. "No more—"

"Running." I kiss him back, pulling him through the entry area to the bed. "So you're not mad at me?"

"I'm livid. I'm starting to believe I have no idea what I'm signing up for with you." He runs a hand roughly through his hair.

"I said I'm—"

"You have to trust me. In this relationship, we are in it together. Waking to an empty bed is a problem."

"I'll leave a note next time."

"No, you will wake me." He cups my chin and what I thought was anger looks more like worry. I've learned my lesson.

I turn my head and kiss his wrist. "I won't do it again." His suspicious eyes meet my pleading ones. "Ever."

He nods and steps back to remove his jacket. I sit on the edge of the bed. Everything is better than I hoped for. Impose Brew signed with S&J. I'm going to submit my letter of resignation from BrandShare when I return home and accept Asher's offer to join the family business. And I have Dylan.

Today is our last day in Dublin. We need to pack. I can't wait to talk to Momma and Asher. But first....

I sit on the edge of the bed reaching for him. His heated gaze is filled with love as he cups my face in his hands. "Happy Birthday Yuki."

"Thank you, Dylan." I kiss him. "I think this was a very successful trip."

"Except for giving me a heart attack, I agree."

"Sorry. I love you. And I think I'm going to love being Dylan's woman."

"I can only think of one thing that's better." He

lowers me to the bed, licking and teasing as he peels away my clothes.

"Better than this?" I pull his body on top of mine.

"Yes, love, and that's being Dylan's wife."

My brother's prediction is right for once in our lives and before Dylan sweeps us away in bliss, I acknowledge without a doubt, "I'm the luckiest woman alive."

THANK you for reading **YUKI'S LUCK**. Yuki and Dylan found their happily ever after. Keep reading as Asher and Jazz experience the highs and lows of love to find their forever love in *Asher's Sonnet.*

Asher Smith is a complicated man. He's hardworking, loving, but distant. And the only way Jasmine Smith can have him fully is to make him think he's lost her for good.

Fed up she asks for a hall pass and he said yes.

Barely holding back her tears, he witnesses the crime scene: her string bikinis, lingerie, and her sexiest f*ck-him dress are packed and aimed to kill.

Jasmine books a flight for a week in Cancun with

Yuki, her friend and his sister, willing to do whatever it takes to get his attention.

This trip will be the death or rebirth of her marriage. It's up to Asher to decide.

Get Your Copy!

SNEAK PEEK! ASHER'S SONNET

ASHER'S STORY

"Can we stay like this forever?" I ask Asher knowing it's impossible. *But a girl can wish, can't I?*

To remain covered in a cocoon of kisses, crazy lovemaking, and the strength of his arms. I could stay in this bed, beneath him, literally until my clock stops ticking. It's irreplaceable.

My sight is blurred as my eyes close letting my fingers paint the picture of him. Asher covers the canvas of my body as my hands traverse the expansion of his moist skin. Slick, smooth, firm, tasty. The muscles in his back flex and relax as his lips explore. Our breathing in sync.

"I believe *that* is the most tempting offer I've had all day. How can I refuse Mrs. Smith?" He grips my lower thighs and wraps my legs around his waist. His gruff chuckle is the only sound I hear as he takes me on a first class trip to heaven and back.

Asher climbs up my body, tossing back the sheets and the breeze from the ceiling fan causes goosebumps to cover my exposed skin, and I shiver as his sweet kisses awaken every part of me.

I love this man.

Hours later I sweep my hand across his side of the bed, and the sheets are cold. A flash of loneliness stabs my heart as I reach for the next best thing, his pillow. I take a deep inhale, glancing over at his nightstand. He always leaves a note.

> *"This is the very ecstasy of love." - WS*
>> *You make it impossible to leave. Will you accept my love as a deposit on our forever?*
>> *Wish me well.*
>> *Love you, My Lady.*

Asher has an old soul, quoting Shakespeare and 90s love songs in his notes belie the dark suits and his towering presence. He makes it nearly impossible to ask for more, but I can't help it.

"Love you too," I whisper to the vacant house.

I close my eyes and pray for him and Dylan as they meet with another realtor this morning. The powerful duo are best friends and planning to open a beer garden. Their concept is unique but will fit perfectly in the urban, yet laid-back Austin down-town scene. I've lost count of the number of meet-ings, the number of disappointments, but today feels different. I'm hoping his faith and belief in his sister Yuki will make this dream for my man a reality. Which reminds me, I need to call her later today to schedule lunch.

I toss back the covers and cross the room, hoping my breakfast isn't too cold. I snag a t-shirt from Asher's drawer and head to the kitchen to see what he prepared this morning. I smell the bacon still lingering in the air. Peaking in the microwave, I spot my plate. *Yep*, bacon, eggs, and waffles.

After nuking it, I reach for a glass and utensils, setting the single place for myself on the island covered with swirling gray marble. The beauty of our home is unmatched. But the open style family kitchen with its stainless steel appliances and black cabinets is unlike any I've ever had in my life.

I look around the room. The drapes, hardwood floors, the immaculate decor are what dreams are made of. I grew up in a working family. Not rich. Not poor. All four of my parents work daily. And I went to college, snagging a job with a startup magazine and immediately joined the ranks of the upper 1% of society until I was replaced.

I retrace my steps back to our room and head to my walk-in closet. It could house a small family. Clothes for every occasion line the walls, as a gift from Asher for my birthday. New floors, new track lighting, cream walls. The island has a chair on one end and drawers on the other. The sides have all types of contraptions holding my jewelry, accessories, and more thingamabobs than I could ever use, *in life*.

I open the second drawer in search of my notebook. The beep of the microwave finds me on all fours reaching in the back. So, I snatch up the book and take it with me, following the sound back to the kitchen. I place it next to my juice and grab my plate from the microwave. I need tape. I deposit my plate on the placemat and get the tape from the side drawer near the door leading to the garage.

I add today's note to the others. I say my grace and dig in flipping through the pages and pages of notes, letters, Asher in written words. On paper, my Shakespeare quoting, cooking man is the epitome of a dream man.

We met in Las Vegas, and before I knew it, I became Mrs. Smith and no longer lived in New York but Austin, Texas. *The boy is bad.* I chew on the bacon searching for the right words. That's kind of what my days are like now. Losing my job, moving to Austin without my family or friends, leaves me endless time to think. To process my thoughts. To pick the moments apart to try to figure out how did *this* all happen.

He swept me off my feet. Dinners and calls and words. It felt like Asher found a way to fill the cracks in my heart. His brooding presence felt like the sun after endless rainy days. And I bloomed under his rays.

We met and dated long distance for less than six months, and we are just shy of the anniversary of that trip. The moment we met. These have been the best and worst days of my life.

I flip a few more pages, brushing the scratch of Asher's penmanship across the back of an envelope. It's like he can't wait to transcribe the thoughts in his head. He grabs whatever, whenever, and composes. An Asher sonnet.

Not fourteen lines.

Not perfect in rhythmic sound.

But a sonnet nonetheless.

And I know I love Asher, and he loves me, but the nagging question of my existence is, *Am I happy?*

Am I, Jasmine Smith, happy? And for the life of

me, I want to say yes. I have every reason to say yes. *Right?*

I finish my breakfast, wash the plate. I return my notebook to its place in the drawer behind my extra sexy lingerie. The quiet of the house affirming yet another day of being alone, waiting for Asher to finish conquering the world.

I can't let the silence consume me.

I, too had my sights set on slaying the world until Swagged Out Style disrupted my global domination. The ring of my phone stops my endless musing.

"What up Tiff?" I head to the living room glad for the distraction.

"You baby! Has Romeo left the building?" Her laughter blends with the hustle and bustle of New York in the background. *I miss it.*

"You know it." I glance at the clock. "He should be meeting with the realtor as we speak."

"Him and that fine ass friend of his."

"Him and Dylan?" I correct her, shaking my head at my best friend. Tiffany is always on one thousand percent. "Yes, girl. They are touring another potential location for Smith & Jameson."

"Bae-bae I'd be down with the swirl for a taste of that one."

I can see her in my mind rolling her neck and

snapping her fingers. And I burst into laughter. We laugh until I'm laid back on the bed wiping away the traces of her exuberance.

"You'd be down with the swirl for Dylan, huh?"

"Yes hunty and I'd become a southern belle, a housewife, I'd kick my man to the curb…all of that."

"Girl, I'm not having this conversation with you. You know your butt ain't leaving New York. And Kevin would follow you."

"Chile' please. Kevin would have to kiss my entire—"

"Tiff!" I cover my mouth to stifle my laughter at her aggressive tone. She means business. A lifetime of friendship tells me so. And those two are always up to something. It is the nature of their relationship. They fight, they make up. They fight, they make up. Today must be a fighting day.

"Don't you Tiff me. I'm tired of Kevin and his hollow promises. Just a second." I hear her mumbling on the other end. I use the time to slip on my jeans and find a clean shirt of my own.

"Sorry," she pops back in, her voice in 'work-mode.' "I will not tell you about Kevin. I'm liable to start cussing and get kicked out of the building. That man knows how to light a fire under my a—"

"Tiffany Ann."

A hoof crossed thousands of miles. "What is wrong with him?"

"I guess men problems are in the water."

"Well, pass me a Dr. Pepper or a shot." Her laugh didn't hold her bubbly personality this time. "I'm tired," she whispered. "And I'm happy for you and your new life but how is it that Asher sees you and puts a ring on it and my man can't see that I want more?"

Boom. Tiffany's whisper found a kindred spirit.

"Tiff, can I help?"

"Yes, hook me up with Dylan." She whines.

"Tiffany I can't with you!" I howl.

"Yes, you can." A door slams in the background on her end. "You got me pouring out my soul, and I almost forgot the reason for my call."

That gets my attention.

"Have you kept up with SOS?"

"No, can't say that I have." I built the digital edition of the magazine only to be replaced by the man I hired and trained. "Should I?"

"A little birdie told me advertising is declining and they're ready to give the golden boy a new address, preferably outside of New York."

"Huh." I slide to the end of the bed. Wesley out means I could be back in. But would I want the job? *Hell yes!*

A raise. The corner office. Back in New York. Suits instead of worn blue jeans. I can see it now.

"What are you thinking over there?" Tiff asks.

"Nothing." I lie. I need to update my resume. Should I send it? No. That would make me look desperate. I make a mental note to update it anyway.

"Yeah right. What's going on with you two? And make it quick, I need to get to work."

"I think I'm experiencing a mid-life crisis. Do women have those? And stop laughing at me."

"Who has a midlife crisis at 27? No. One." She laughs so hard it almost hurts my feelings. "Girl you better get your butt up off that plush couch and find something to do. You obviously got too much time on your hands. A midlife crisis." Tiffany laughs totally forgetting she's at work.

"I could use your support Tiff." I wonder if I should slip on workout clothes instead. I'm sure I can't fit my suits anymore.

"Girl I got your front and your back. What's got you tripping?"

"I don't know, I feel like this life isn't my life. Asher works all day and night. And I'm here." I glance around with only the echo of my voice to keep me company. " I miss color and design. Meetings and luncheons. Creativity." That's what I miss most.

"And what does Asher have to say about all of this?"

"He's busy with Smith & Jameson." An antsy feeling gathers in the pit of my stomach. I need to plan a trip. Somewhere different, new.

"Are you still tripping with that man?"

"Don't start Tiff. As a matter of fact, I think I'll plan us an anniversary trip."

"Anniversary?"

"The anniversary of the day we met. Why didn't I think about that before?" I say the last part more to myself. Not Las Vegas again. I walk to the mirror and inspect my reflection. Turning side to side. "Where did you guys go last?"

"Cancun. You'd love it there. Now you're thinking. Go on Stella. Get your groove back. Look I gotta go, the man is calling."

I stand unmoved staring at my reflection. Cancun and Asher in his swim trunks. Images of his chocolate skin stretched out in the white sand. Yeah, us away on a romantic trip is exactly what I need to get my—*no, our*—groove back.

I strut to my closet and pull out a new, sexy tan string bikini. Against my skin, I'll appear almost nude. I do some digging and find the perfect spot for our trip. By the end of the day, I've reserved a condo with a private beach for a week. We'll have plenty of time to explore each other. But first I've got to peel my man away from Smith & Jameson. I'm up for the task. I dangle the fabric in the air. Asher won't be able to resist *this*.

~

Continue Reading...

DEAR READER....

I stumbled on a video on YouTube and it kept me glued to my computer screen. A couple, an African American woman and Korean man, shared their hardships stemming from his family's disapproval of his chosen bride. And a seed was planted. What if, you had a child, a product of such a relationship?

That give me my first brush with a character I'd later name Yuki Smith. Then came Asher, and finally Momma—Rhonda Smith. So this is why this story does not include an Epilogue.

I hope you enjoyed getting to know the Smith family and look forward to the final installments of this shorter series.

Happy Reading,

Ja'Nese Dixon

www.janesedixon.com

Be the FIRST to know!

Join My Newsletter

http://www.janesedixon.com/subscribe

Be the first to know about releases and specials. You can unsubscribe anytime.

KEEP YOUR KINDLE BLAZIN'

Black Stallion Ranch (Contemporary Romance)

Dad Bod Bestie

More Than Love

Finding Love in Italy

Blind to the Truth

Blazin' Love (Contemporary Romance)

Complete Series

Platinum Love (Book 1)

Privileged Love (Book 2)

Exclusive Love (Book 3)

Chosen Love (Book 4)

Special Love (Book 5)

Absolute Love (Book 6)

Pretend for Me (A Short Story)

Devoted Love (Book 7)

Select Love (Book 8)

Lavish Love (Book 9)

Total Love (Book 10)

Forbidden Chords Series (Contemporary Romance)

Complete Series

Hidden Desire (Prequel)

Rockstar Seduction (Prequel)

Rockstar Secrets (Book 1)

Rockstar Sinners (Book 2)

Rockstar Savages (Book 3)

Waiting for You (A Short Story)

This Song's for You (A Short Story)

Rockstar Scandals (Book 4)

Secret Soulmates Boxed Set (Books 1 - 3)

Misfits (Steamy Romance)

Thrice the Dare

Precious Stones Series (Romantic Suspense)

Before Black Diamond (Prequel)

Black Diamond (Book 1)

African Emerald (Book 2)

Fire Opal (Book 3)

Southern Gentlemen (Slow Burn Steamy Romance)

Play to Win (Book 1)

All Yours (Book 2)

Honest and True (Book 3)

Game Over (Book 4)

Full Rush (Book 5)

Fair Catch (Book 6)

Rules of Love (Book 7)

Smith Pact Duo (Contemporary Romance)

Complete Series

Yuki's Luck (Book 1)

Tempting Asher (Book 2)

Smith Surprise (Book 3)

When It Comes to Love Boxed Set (Books 1 - 3)

Weekend Reads

Resort to Love

You Owe Me

Grown and Sexy for Christmas

Preach

Serial Fiction

Secret Desires

See all of my books on my website:

http://www.janesedixon.com/books.

ABOUT THE AUTHOR

USA Today Bestseller, Ja'Nese Dixon writes tales of romance laced with strong women, stronger men, and family values that are based on more than blood. Her happily ever afters are written to inspire. So, if you're looking for a page turner that will leave you blushing, with your heart racing, and lying to yourself about reading "just one more chapter" then grab one of the author's thirty-something books.

Ja'Nese is an avid reader and coffee drinker living in Houston, TX with her husband, three adult children, and her spoiled diva dog. Want to learn more? Join her newsletter and get exclusive reads, all the inside details, and a first look at what's to come at www.janesedixon.com.

Stay in Touch:
www.janesedixon.com
info@janesedixon.com

amazon.com/author/janesedixon

bookbub.com/authors/ja-nese-dixon

goodreads.com/janese_dixon

facebook.com/AuthorJaNeseDixon

instagram.com/authorjanesedixon

ABOUT THE PUBLISHER

Purpose Prevails Publishing
2231B Center St. STE 144
Deer Park, TX 77536
www.purposeprevailspublishing.com

Get Pretend for Me for FREE!

Here's another sweet, steamy romance for your device.

https://geni.us/pretendformegift